P9-DIW-552

For Eleanor, Lizzie, and Andrew

Published by Bloomsbury Publishing, New York and London
Distributed to the trade by Holtzbrinck Publishers

Library of Congress Cataloging-in-Publication Data
Archer, Dosh.
Looking after little Ellie / written and illustrated by Dosh and Mike Archer.—1st U.S. ed.
p. cm.
Summary: Six small mice have their paws full when they babysit one large baby elephant.
ISBN-10: 1-58234-971-1
ISBN-13: 978-1-58234-971-8
[1. Size—Fiction. 2. Babysitters—Fiction. 3. Babies—Fiction. 4. Mice—Fiction.
5. Elephants—Fiction.] I. Archer, Mike, ill. II. Title.
PZ7.A6745Lo 2005 [E]—dc22 2004054733

First U.S. Edition 2005
Printed in Singapore
1 3 5 7 9 10 8 6 4 2

Bloomsbury Publishing, Children's Books, U.S.A.
175 Fifth Avenue
New York, NY 10010

All papers used by Bloomsbury Publishing are natural, recyclable products made from wood grown in well-managed forests. The manufacturing processes conform to the environmental regulations of the country of origin.

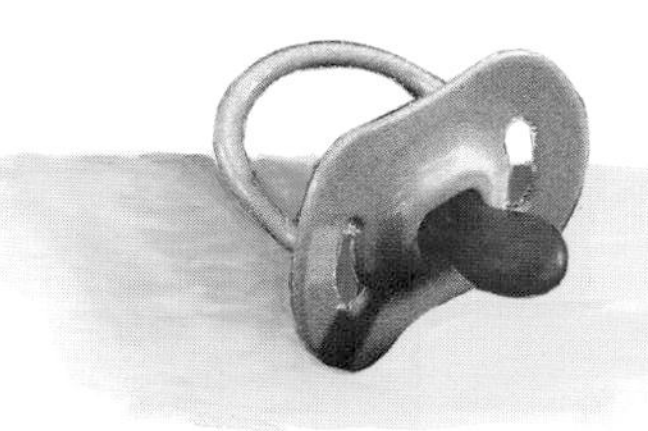

Looking After Little Ellie

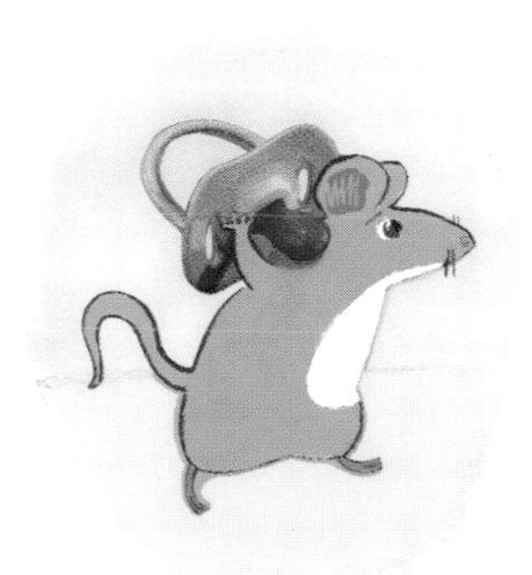

written and illustrated by
Dosh and Mike Archer

When Flora called to ask us to
look after Little Ellie, we said yes.
After all, you have to help your friends.

It was the first time we had looked after Little Ellie.

Flora said she would be back soon.

But when her mother left,
Little Ellie got a bit upset.

So we did our best to cheer her up.

We gave her
some lunch,

changed her diaper,

and took her to the park.

We played on the swing . . .

... and the seesaw.

We sang for her and danced for her,

and then she had a nap.
She looked really sweet
when she was asleep.

Then it was time to go home.

When she got back, Flora said,
"I hope Little Ellie hasn't been any trouble."

"Not a bit," we said as we kissed Little Ellie good-bye.

It was a big day, but we didn't mind.
After all, she was just a little baby.